LET'S GET TO KNOW OUR FEELINGS

THIS BOOK BELONGS TO

© 2021, Kids Castle Press. All rights reserved. No part of this publication may be reproduced, stored, distributed, or transmitted, in any form or by means, including photocopying, recording, or other electronic or mechanical methods, without prior written permission of the publisher, except in the case of brief quotations embodied in critical reviews and certain other noncommercial uses permitted by copyright law.

When my friend takes my soccer ball without asking for it first...

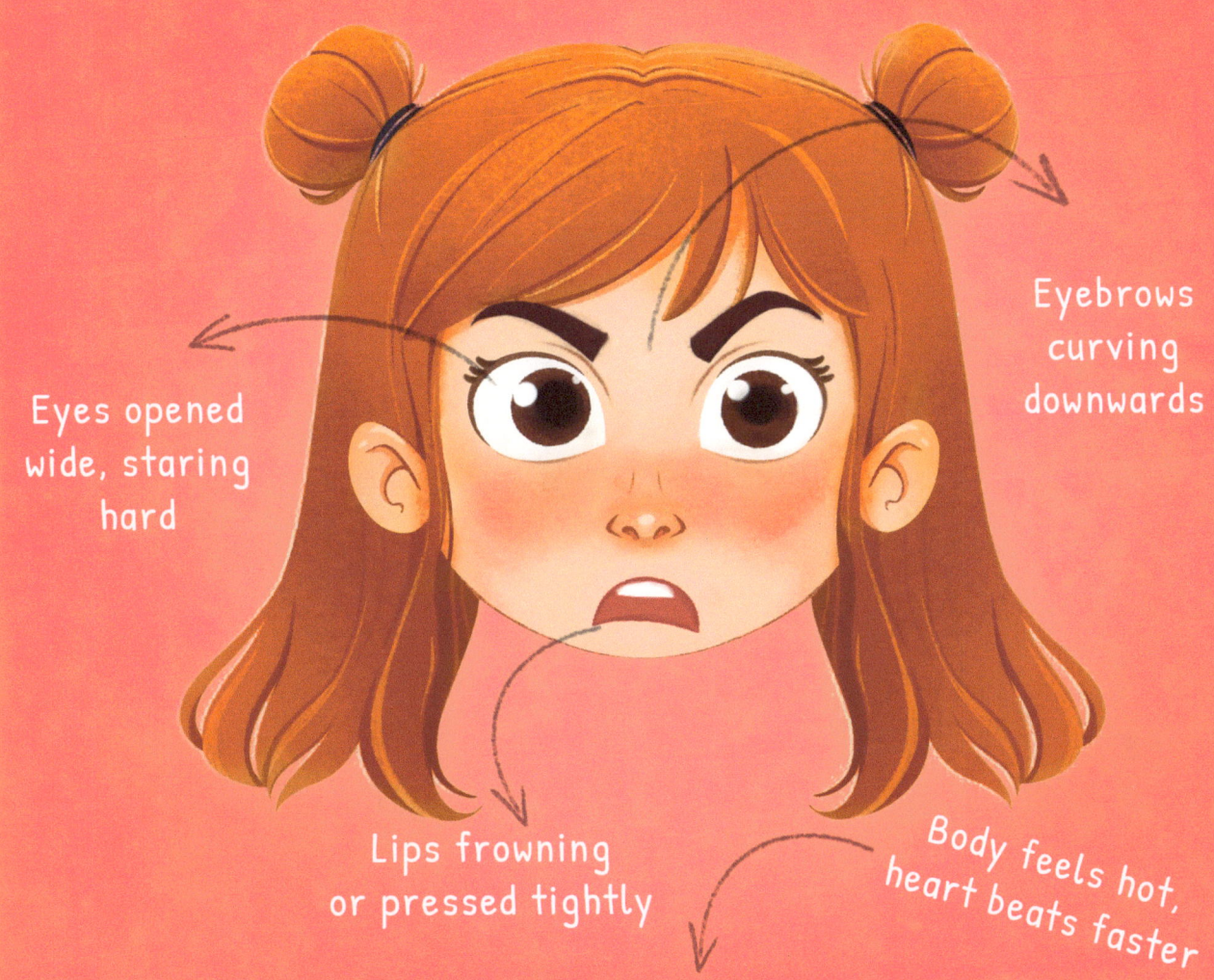

When Mommy says she'll be right back and goes away...

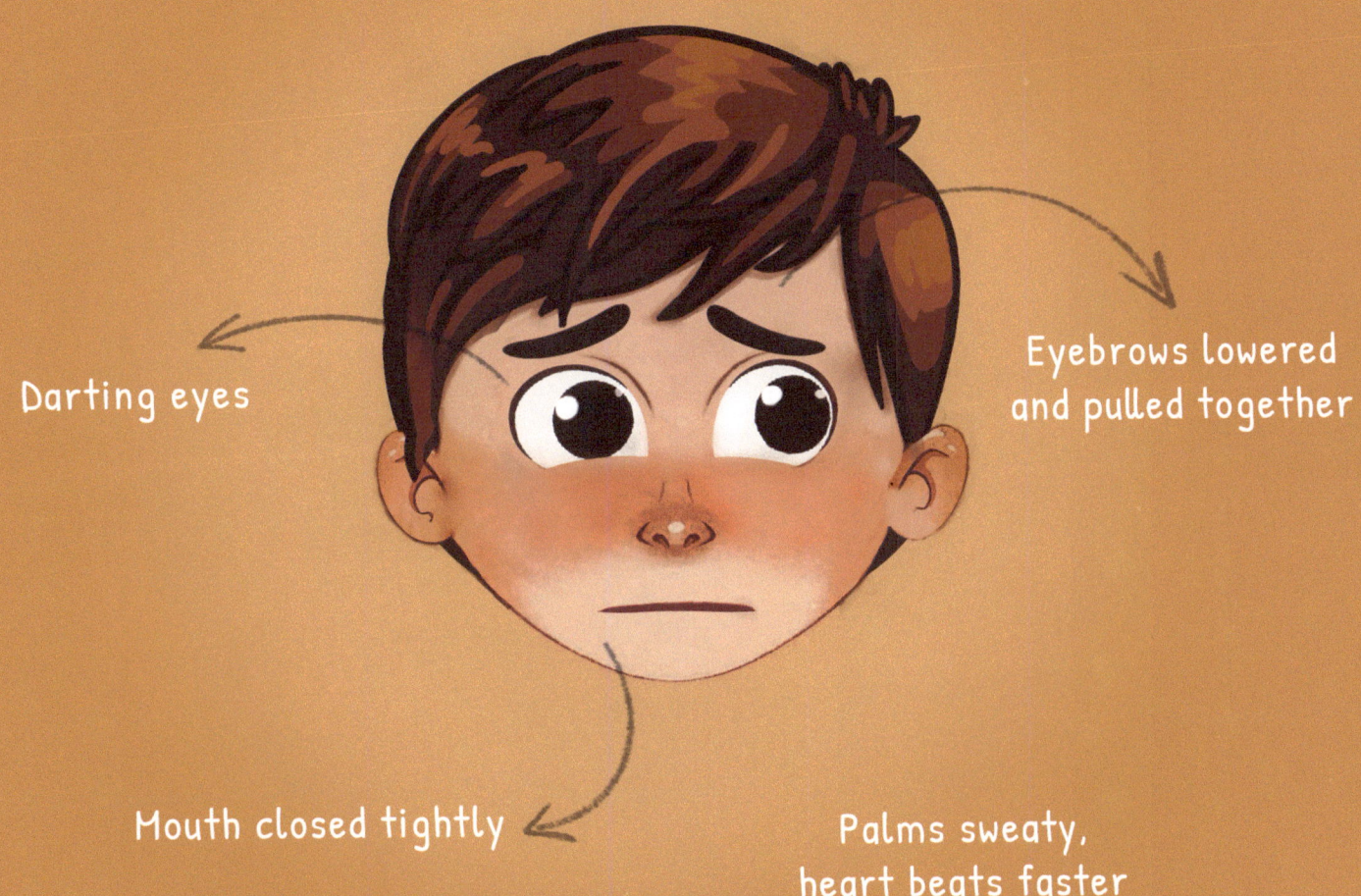

When I've practiced hard and believe that I can win the race...

When my teacher asks me a question that I don't know the answer to...

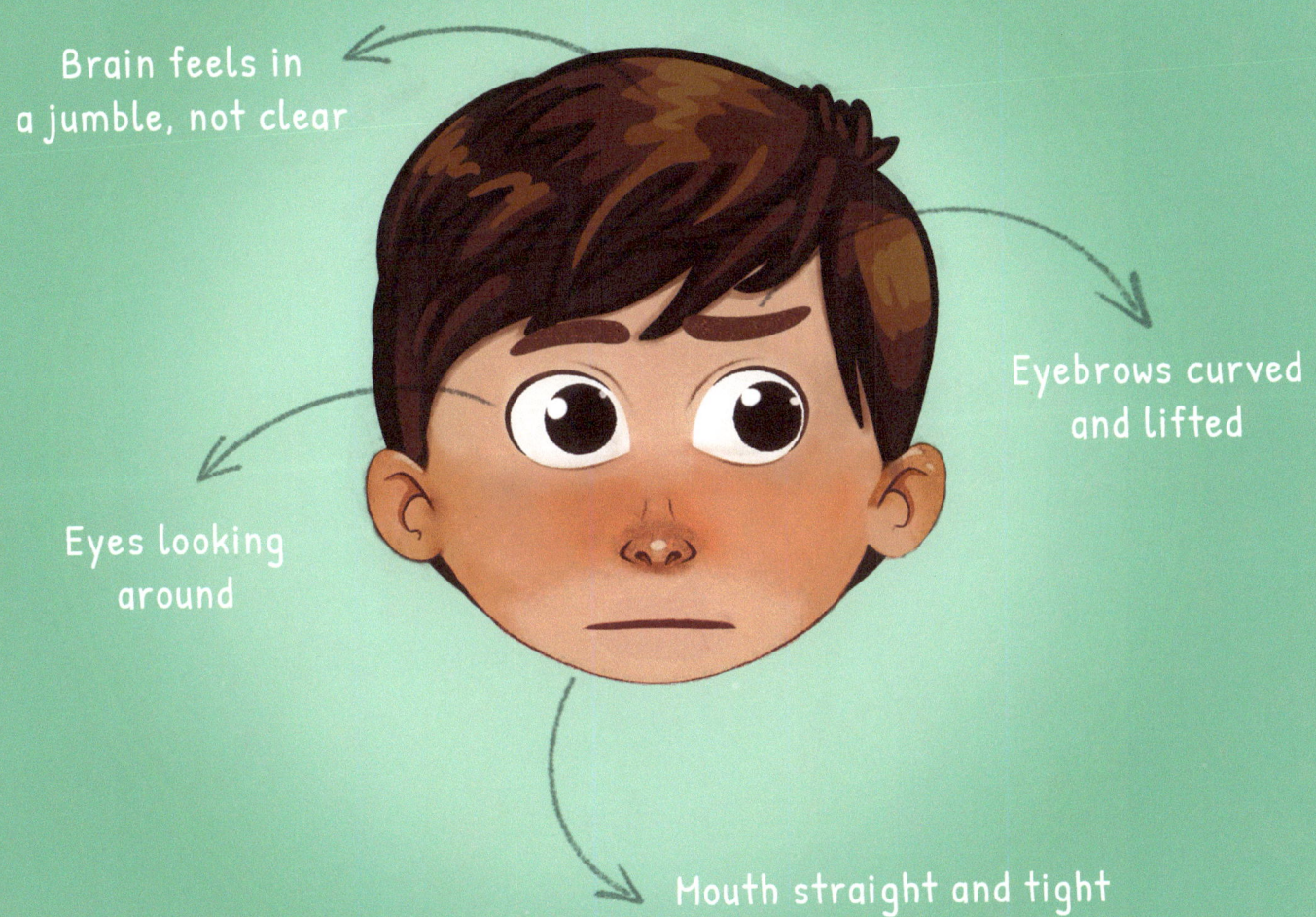

When our teacher says she has something new to teach us...

When I trip in front of my friends...

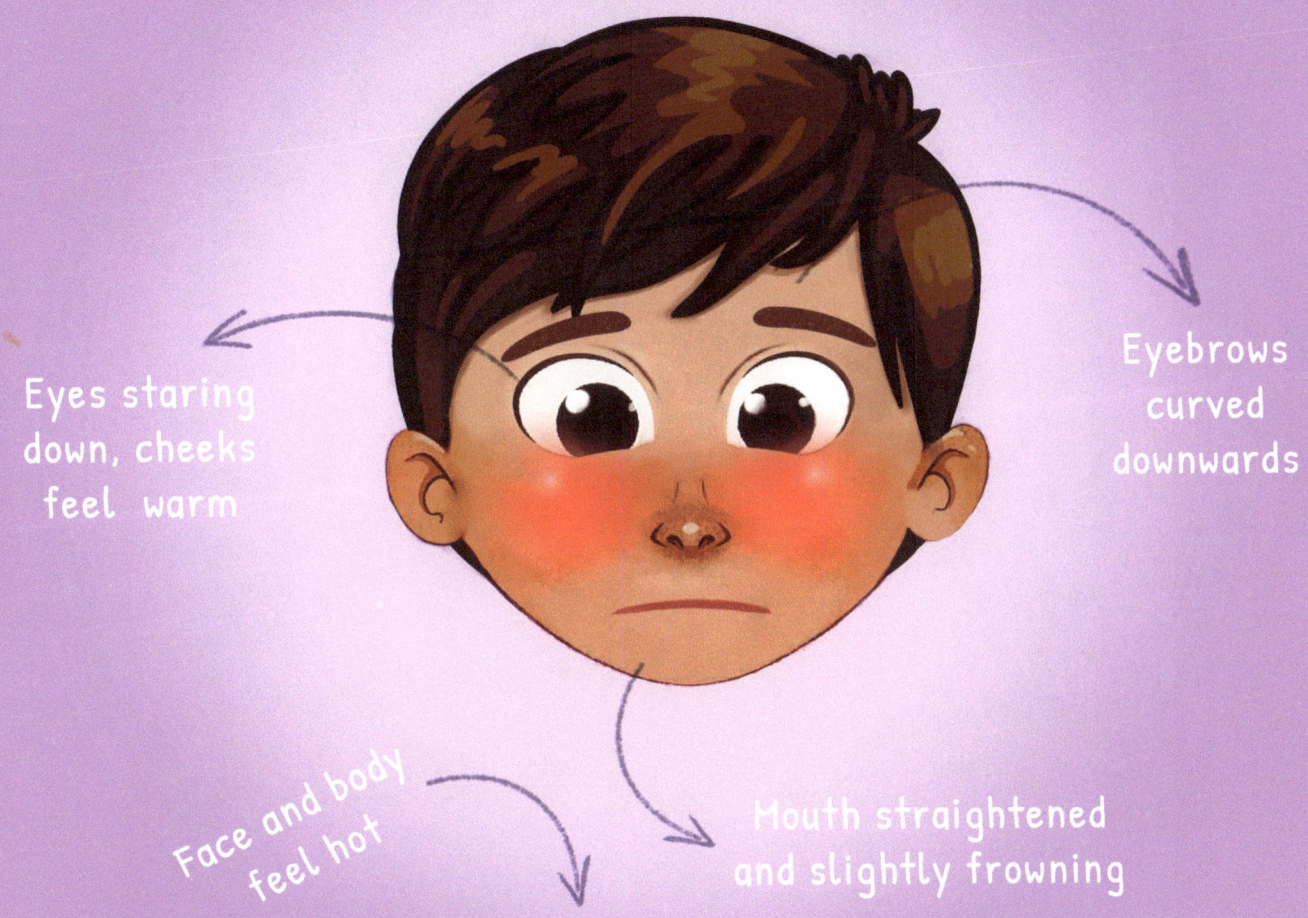

When my best friend and I are jumping around the playground...

I FEEL EXCITED

Eyes sparkling and wide open

Eyebrows lifted high

Mouth open in enthusiasm

Heart beats faster, body wants to move around

AND IT'S OKAY TO FEEL THIS WAY!

When I want something,
but no one is paying attention to me...

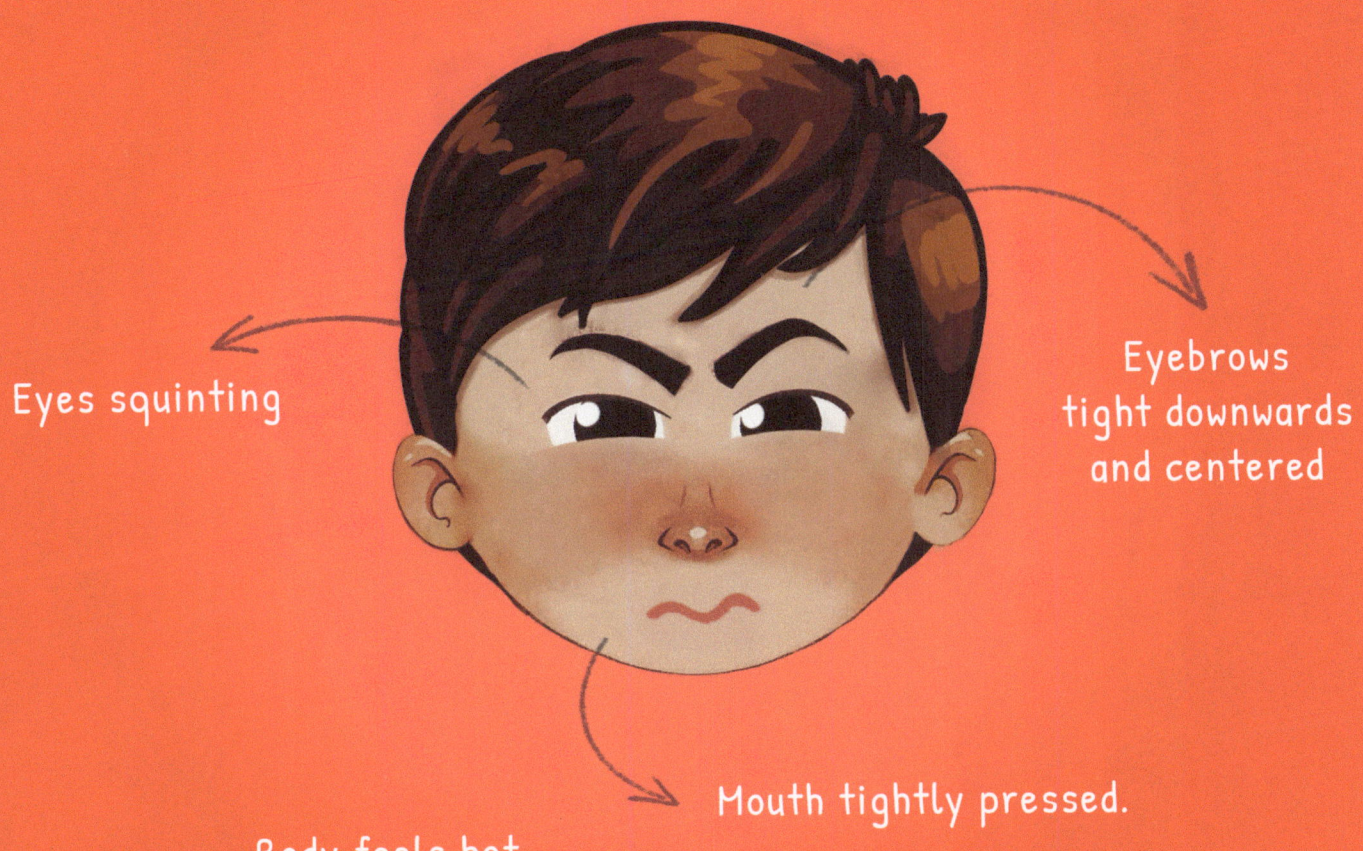

WHAT CAN I DO
WHEN I FEEL ANGRY OR FRUSTRATED?

1 Take deep breaths! In, out, in out...

2 Tell someone you trust why I feel this way!

USEFUL TIP

WHAT CAN I DO
WHEN I FEEL EXCITED OR HAPPY?

1 Feel grateful!

2 Share the happy news with my best friend!

USEFUL TIP

WHAT CAN I DO
WHEN I FEEL CURIOUS?

1. Investigate!
2. Ask questions!

USEFUL TIP

WHAT CAN I DO
WHEN I FEEL EMBARRASSED?

1. Laugh it off!
2. It's happened to everyone.

USEFUL TIP

When I've broken a glass vase...

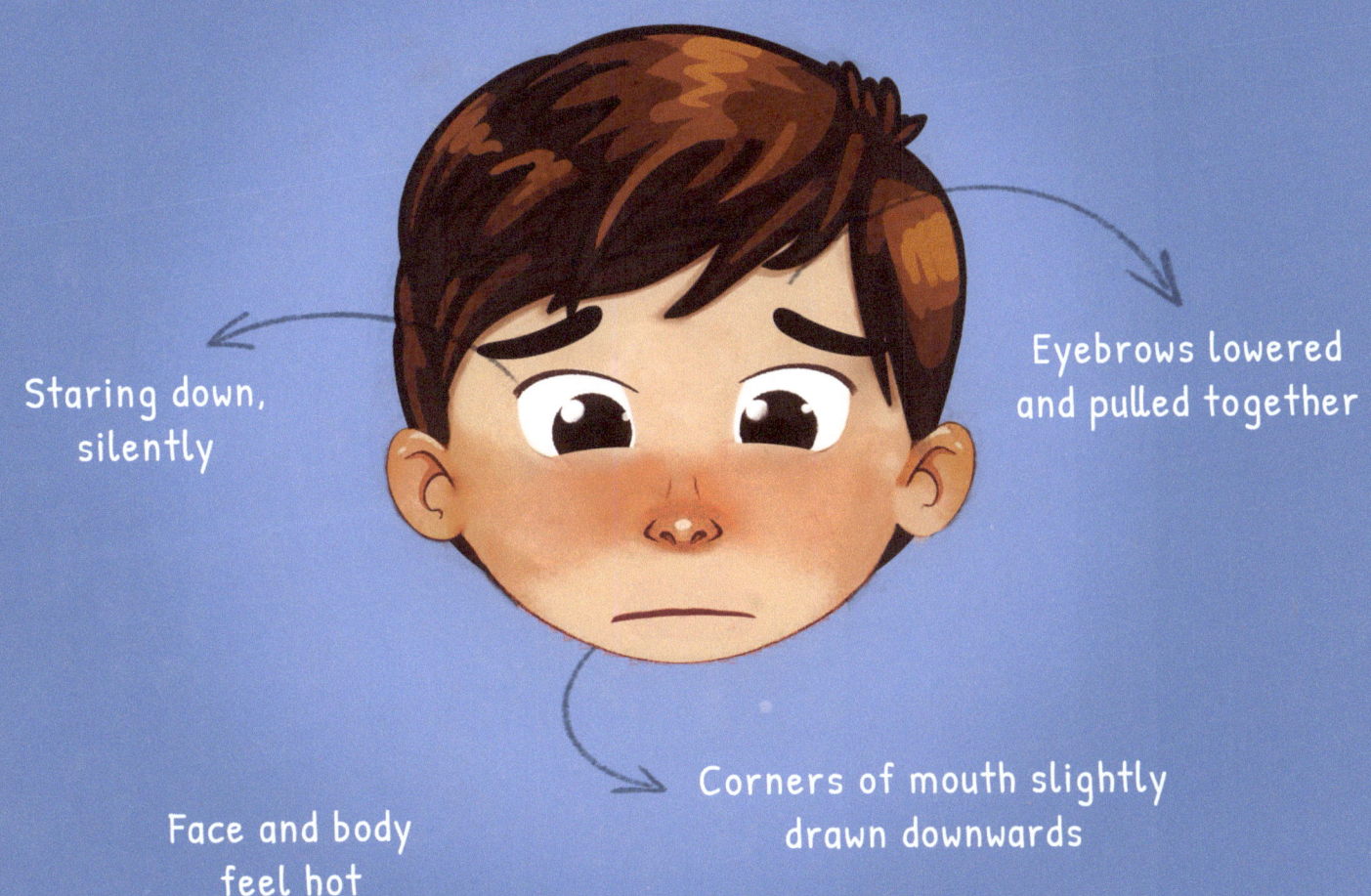

When I'm dancing to my favorite song...

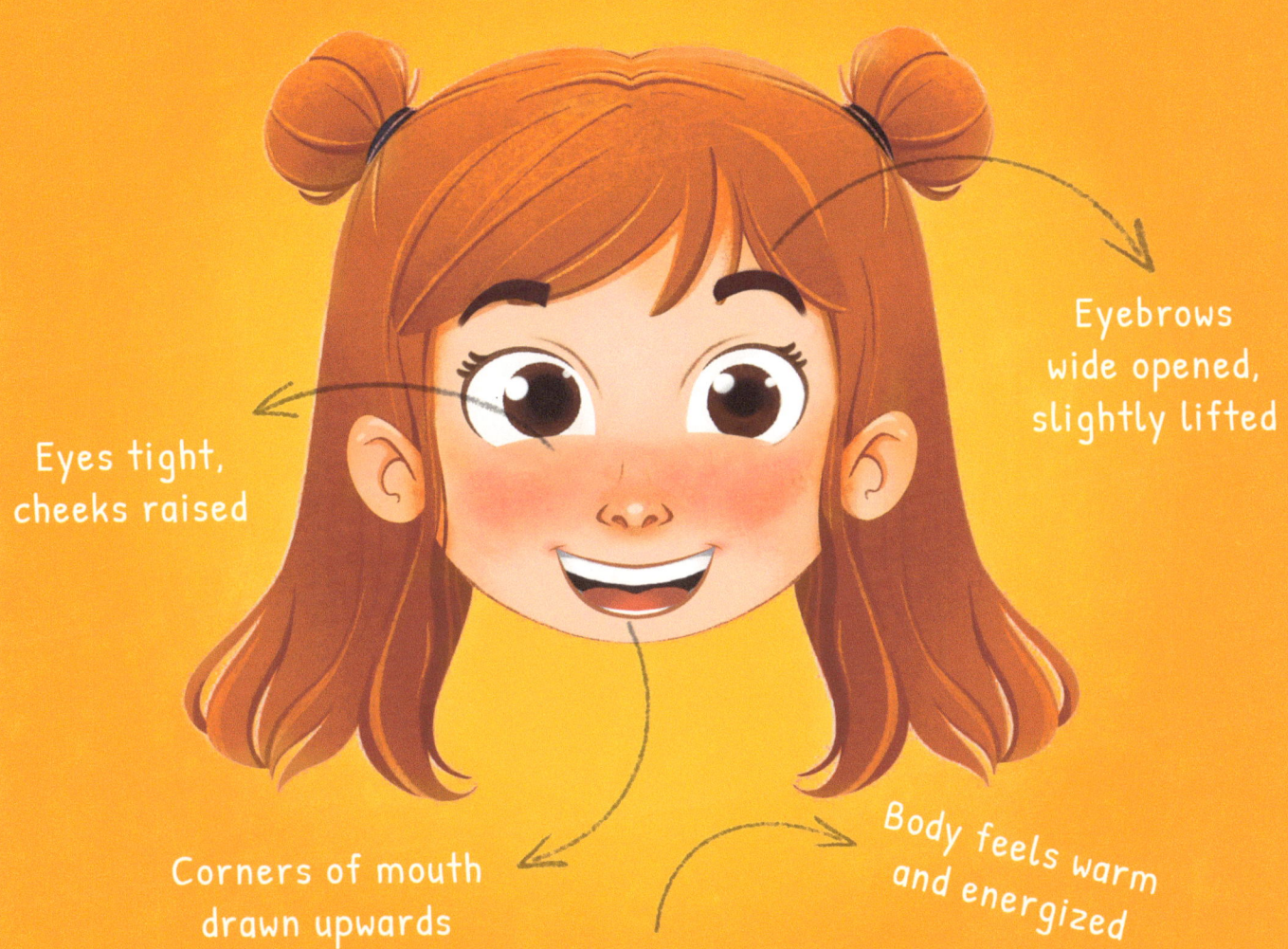

When my friend has got
the bigger lollipop...

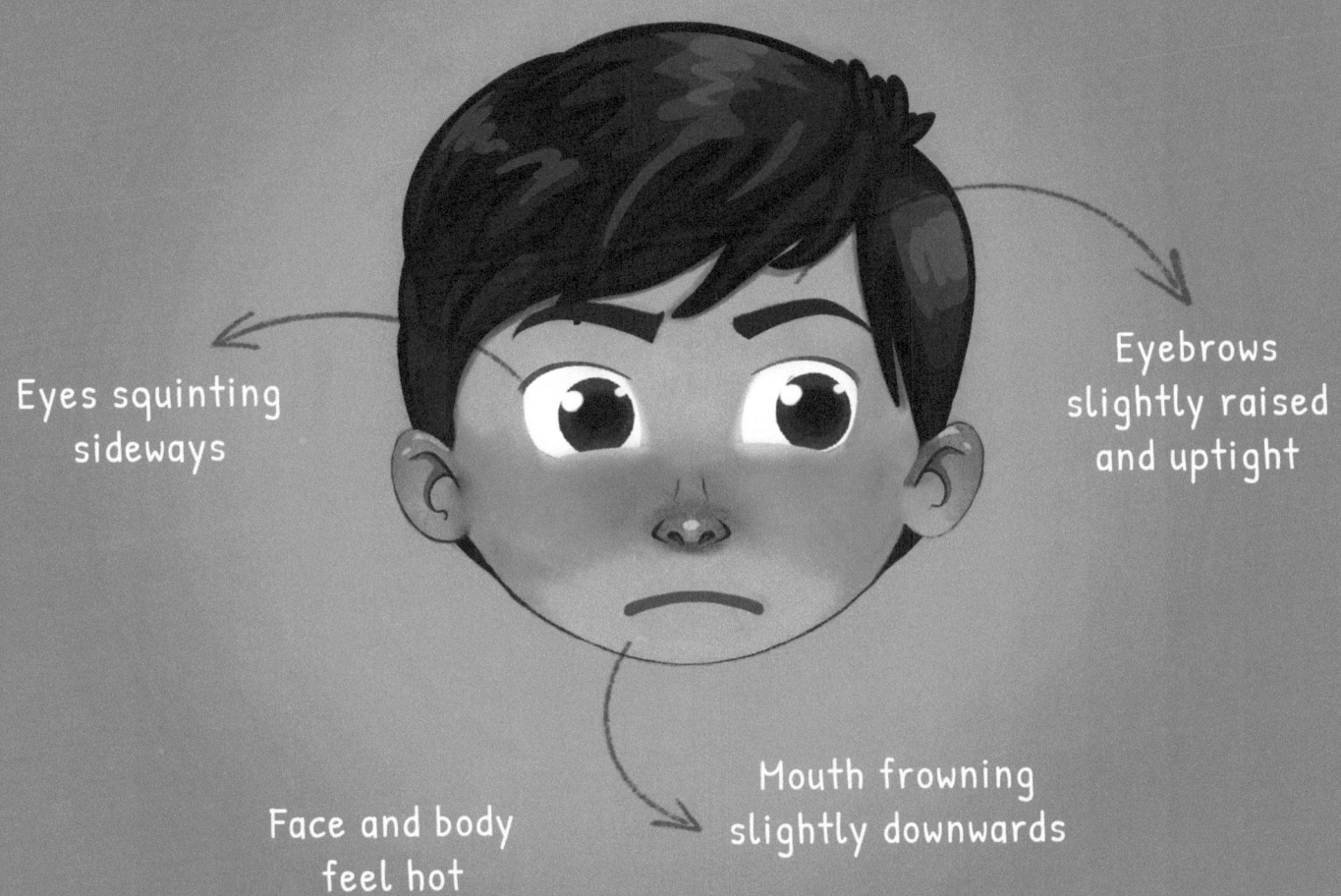

When I hug my dog...

When I accidentally dropped my ice cream right after buying it...

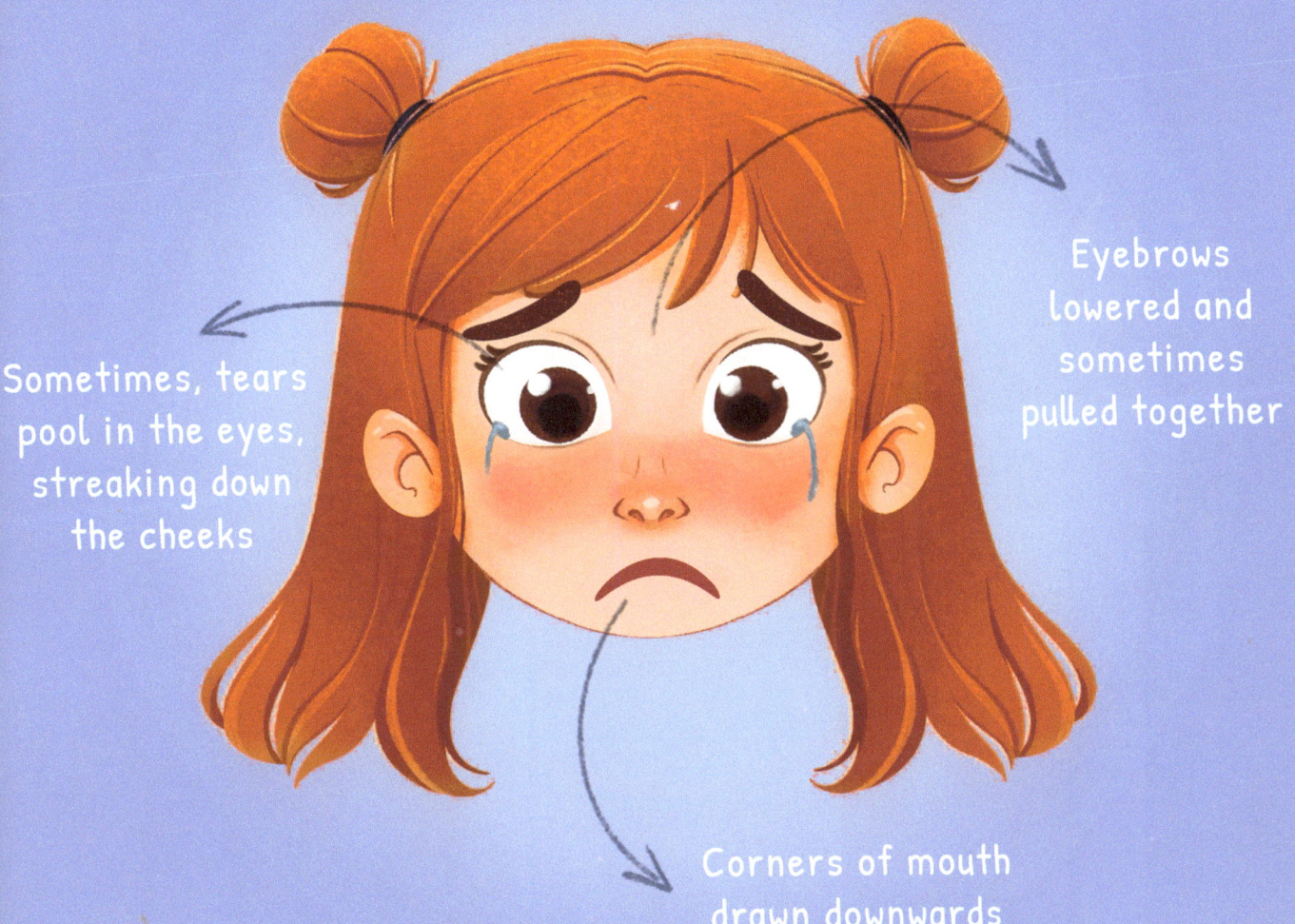

WHAT CAN I DO
WHEN I FEEL GUILTY?

1 Tell someone you trust why you feel this way

2 Apologize if you did something wrong, and learn from what happened!

USEFUL TIP

WHAT CAN I DO
WHEN I FEEL SAD?

1 Express it by crying, drawing, or being alone with your thoughts – whatever you need!

2 Talk to someone you trust about why you feel this way!

USEFUL TIP

WHAT CAN I DO
WHEN I FEEL JEALOUS?

1 Tell someone you trust why you feel that way.

2 Think of the bright side of what you have, and what's special and positive about it!

USEFUL TIP

WHAT CAN I DO
WHEN I FEEL WORRIED?

1 Take deep breaths! In, out, in, out...

2 Know that I'm safe right now.

USEFUL TIP

When I wake up from a nightmare..

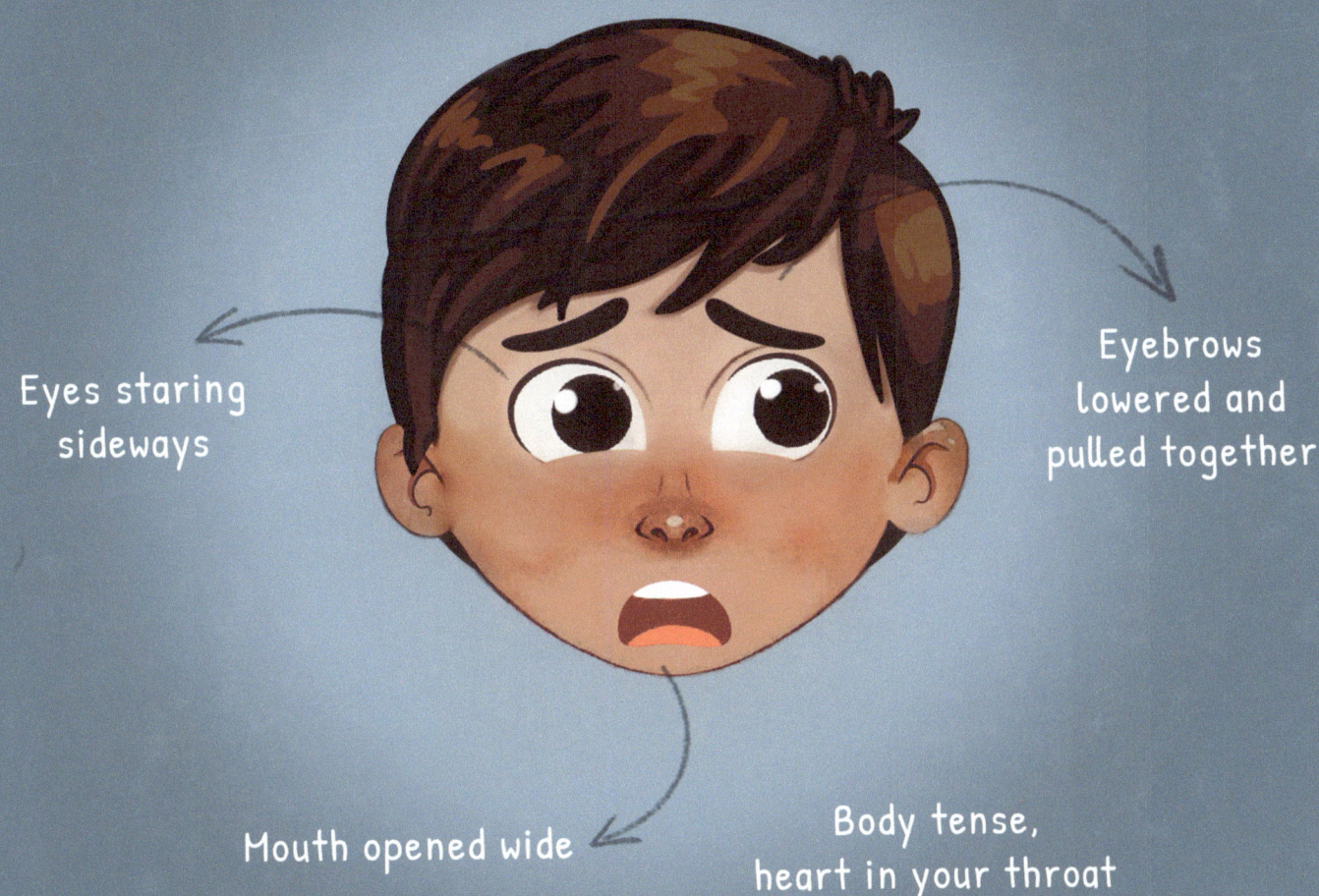

When my friend introduces me
to the new girl in our school...

When my friends suddenly sing
"Happy Birthday" to me...

THANK YOU FOR LEARNING ABOUT FEELINGS WITH US!

CPSIA information can be obtained
at www.ICGtesting.com
Printed in the USA
LVHW072106161121
703476LV00016B/372